This book is dedicated to:

Leo and Ross...my two sweet boys.
You are the light of my life.

My Mom...Thank you Momma for all of
your love and support. I am the
mother I am because of you.

And Arturo...I love doing life with
you. Thank you for always being my
biggest cheerleader.

MY MOMMY & DADDY ARE
RANCHERS

Hi! I am Leo and this is my brother Ross!

My mommy and daddy are ranchers.

They drop my brother and I off at school
in their cowboy boots and spurs.

When they meet my friends,
my friends always ask,
"Are they REAL cowboys?"

While we are at school, Mommy and Daddy ride their horses, Super and Holly, through the pasture to check on the cows that are grazing on the green grass.

Mommy and Daddy make sure
the cows are happy and not sick.

Then they pick us up from school
and we go home to unsaddle Super and Holly.

I help give the horses a bath
and my brother feeds them
their grain for supper.

Then it's our turn for a bath and supper!
Tonight it is spaghetti and meatballs, our favorite!

My mommy and daddy are ranchers.

In the winter, we all bundle up
to go feed the cows every day.

We put grain in the bunk and count the cows as they come in for their breakfast.

Then we go put out hay,
so the cows have a snack after breakfast.

When we are done, we come in for a hot chocolate break!

My mommy and daddy are ranchers, and they care for me, my brother, and our cows every day!

I want to be a rancher one day too!

CLASSIC SPAGHETTI AND MEATBALLS

For more recipes from Wrenn and her family,
visit their food blog www.cookingwiththecowboy.com.

INGREDIENTS

1 lb ground beef	1 medium onion diced
1/4 cup grated parmesan	4 cloves garlic minced
1/2 cup breadcrumbs	2 carrots peeled
4 tbsp pesto	2 celery
4 tbsp tomato paste	2 14.5 oz can diced tomatoes
1 egg	salt and pepper

INSTRUCTIONS

Begin by coating the skillet with olive oil. Sauté half a medium onion. Add the 1 tbsp of tomato paste and 2 cloves of the garlic and cook down for a minute or two. Once they are cooked down remove from skillet and place in a bowl to combine with the ground beef for the meatballs.

To make the meatballs, combine the ground beef, half of the pesto and sautéed onions, breadcrumbs, egg, and parmesan. Then form meatballs about the size of an egg and you will end up with about twelve meatballs.

Add your puree of carrots, onion, and celery in the same pot and don't worry about scraping out the bits of meatballs left, as it will only give the puree more flavor.

Stir the puree to deglaze the pan and cook down until the vegetables stick to the pan and then add 3 tbsp of tomato paste. Cook 1-2 minutes.

Then add the tomatoes, salt, and pepper. Stir and let come to a simmer. Add the remainder of the pesto.

Then add the meatballs back in the pot and cook for 10 minutes or so until the meatballs are done.

Serve over your pasta of choice and enjoy!

Photographs by Megan Hein of Megan Hein Photography

Thank you for reading **My Mommy and Daddy are Ranchers.** This book is near and dear to my heart and I hope that you and your family have enjoyed reading it as much as I enjoyed writing it.

Love,

Wrenn

ABOUT THE AUTHOR

Wrenn Pacheco is the mother of two little cowboys, Leo and Ross. She is a professional photographer and also works as a rancher with her husband, Arturo, in the Flint Hills of Kansas. In their operation, they care for double stock yearlings and develop heifers. Wrenn was inspired to write this book by watching her sons grow up in the ranching life.

To connect with Wrenn and her family you can find them on Instagram @cookingwiththecowboy.

ABOUT THE ARTIST

Abra Shirley grew up on a farm in northeast Kansas, and graduated from the University of Kansas in May of 2020. She is currently working as a freelance artist specializing in children's book illustration and commissioned fine art.

To see more artwork or connect with Abra, visit her website at www.artbyabra.com.

Photography Credit
Many thanks to Wrenn Pacheco, Scott Stebner, and Megan Hein, whose photographs helped to inspire some of the illustrations in this book.

Made in the USA
Monee, IL
17 January 2021